TAKING CARE OF WHERE WE LIVE

*Question, connect and take action to become better citizens
with a brighter future. Now that's smart thinking!*

TAKING CARE OF WHERE WE LIVE

RESTORING ECOSYSTEMS

MERRIE-ELLEN WILCOX

ILLUSTRATED BY
AMANDA KEY

ORCA BOOK PUBLISHERS

Published in Canada and the United States in 2024 by Orca Book Publishers.
orcabook.com

Library and Archives Canada Cataloguing in Publication
Title: Taking care of where we live : restoring ecosystems / Merrie-Ellen Wilcox ; illustrated by Amanda Key.
Names: Wilcox, Merrie-Ellen, author. | Key, Amanda, illustrator.
Series: Orca think ; 17.
Description: Series statement: Orca think ; 17 | Includes bibliographical references and index.
Identifiers: Canadiana (print) 20230562833 | Canadiana (ebook) 20230562841 | ISBN 9781459835382 (hardcover) | ISBN 9781459835399 (PDF) | ISBN 9781459835405 (EPUB)
Subjects: LCSH: Restoration ecology—Juvenile literature. | LCSH: Restoration ecology—Citizen participation—Juvenile literature. | LCGFT: Instructional and educational works.
Classification: LCC QH541.15.R45 W55 2024 | DDC j333.71/53—dc23

Library of Congress Control Number: 2023948934

Summary: Part of the nonfiction Orca Think series for middle-grade readers, this illustrated book introduces readers to ecological restoration and what they can do to help ecosystems in their own communities and around the world.

Orca Book Publishers is committed to reducing the consumption of nonrenewable resources in the production of our books. We make every effort to use materials that support a sustainable future.

Orca Book Publishers gratefully acknowledges the support for its publishing programs provided by the following agencies: the Government of Canada, the Canada Council for the Arts and the Province of British Columbia through the BC Arts Council and the Book Publishing Tax Credit.

Cover and interior artwork by Amanda Key
Design by Troy Cunningham
Edited by Kirstie Hudson

Printed and bound in South Korea.

27   26   25   24   •   1   2   3   4

For everyone, young and old,
who is helping to restore this beautiful
planet that we all call home

CONTENTS

INTRODUCTION

Early one morning many years ago, several Garry oak trees were cut down to make way for a hospital parking lot at the end of my street. Many people had been opposed to cutting the trees, so the job was done at dawn, before anyone knew what was happening. Garry oaks are the centerpiece of an **ecosystem** that once dominated southern Vancouver Island, where I am lucky enough to live. Besides being huge and beautiful—and centuries old—each of the trees provided **habitat** and food for countless birds and insects. I didn't know it at the time, but the anger and sadness I felt that morning would set me on a path to learning how we can start to make things right. I hope you'll join me on that path and become part of #GenerationRestoration!

Garry oak trees, young and old, in a meadow in springtime.
CHRISTA BOAZ/GETTY IMAGES

1

JUST ONE AMONG MILLIONS

Scientists estimate that there are about 8.7 million species of living things—including plants, animals, fungi, bacteria and other microorganisms—on this beautiful blue planet we call Earth. And we humans, known as *Homo sapiens*, are just one of them. We are as dependent on our earthly environment as all the other species. We cannot survive without the food, water, oxygen, light, warmth and other essentials that Earth provides. We live in a web of relationships with everything else in the natural world.

Unlike all those other species, though, humans have damaged the planet on which we depend for our survival. For thousands of years, we have been altering nature in various ways—for example, by clearing land in order to grow plants

Almost 95 percent of Earth's surface has been changed by humans, whether through development, agriculture, transportation, mining, production or distribution of energy—or several of these at once.

MYKHAILO PAVLENKO/SHUTTERSTOCK.COM

and keep animals for food, changing the paths of streams and rivers to water our crops, and using fire to improve the soil.

But in the last 600 years, with the massive growth of our population, our impacts on nature have exploded as well. Not only do we need to feed, clothe and house everyone, but those of us in wealthier countries consume far more of everything than we need. In fact, we now consume more than the planet can provide for us and produce more waste than it can absorb.

We overharvest, taking too many trees and too many fish. We dam rivers to generate electricity. We cut down forests, fill in or drain important **wetlands** and convert **grasslands** to grow food and build cities. We fill the ocean with plastic. We pollute the air, water and soil with our own waste and with chemicals. There is no place on the planet that we haven't damaged in one way or another. And, of course, we've even changed the climate. In short, we've made a really big mess.

PUTTING OUR BEST FOOT FORWARD

Homo sapiens means "intelligent or wise human." Clearly, we've been neither intelligent nor wise when it comes to

WILD IDEA

Since the 1970s, humans have been consuming more resources than the planet provides each year and producing more waste than it can absorb. Today it takes 1.7 Earths to produce the resources we consume and absorb the waste we produce. Another way to think about this is that it now takes Earth one year and eight months to generate what we consume and produce in one year.

EARTH CAPACITY

RESOURCES REQUIRED

WILD IDEA

Our impact on Earth is so big that some people now call the age we are living in the Anthropocene (from the Greek *anthropo* for "human" and *cene* for "new"), meaning a period when, for the first time, human activities are affecting the whole planet.

taking care of Earth. But we still have a chance. By putting all of our best human qualities to work—our intelligence and wisdom, our knowledge and energy, our passion and commitment—we can restore some of the damage we've done and make the planet healthy once again. The United Nations Decade on ***Ecosystem Restoration*** began in 2021, with the aim of reversing the ***degradation*** of ecosystems on every continent and in every ocean. That in turn will help to combat ***climate change***, prevent the extinction of large numbers of species (***mass extinction***) and reduce poverty. Those are big goals, so everyone will need to step up.

Taking Care of Where We Live is about the ways in which people can (and must) help repair this beautiful planet and how we can all do our part. If you're wondering what

ecosystem restoration even means, don't worry! We'll start by defining ecosystems and why they're important, and then look at the different ways in which they can be restored.

Some of the information in this book is scientific. Other parts of the book are closer to philosophy, thinking about how we look at the world and why things are the way they are. Some of the facts are hard, and even sad, but we need all the knowledge available to us in order to understand what's happening to the planet and what we can do about it. Hope lies in taking action. And action starts from knowledge. So let's get going!

WILD IDEA

The purpose of the UN Decade on Ecosystem Restoration is "to prevent, halt, and reverse the degradation of ecosystems on every continent and in every ocean. It can help to end poverty, combat climate change and prevent a mass extinction."

HOW DID WE GET HERE?

Have you ever wondered how or why we find ourselves in this race against climate change and mass extinction? Most of us are just living our lives, going to school or work, doing our chores, doing our best. We're not out there purposely destroying the planet—although things that many of us take for granted, from buying fish at the grocery store to owning one or more electronic devices, are part of the problem. So how did we get here?

"FILL THE EARTH AND SUBDUE IT"

At one time, most human cultures saw themselves as part of nature, depending on it for almost every aspect of their lives. Many Indigenous Peoples continue to have this kind of relationship with the natural world.

But around 3,000 years ago, when the **book of Genesis** was written, a new idea began to take root. The book told humans to "fill the earth and subdue it" and to "rule over the fish in the sea and the birds in the sky and over every living creature that moves on the ground." The Christian belief in life after death, which came a few hundred years later, also meant that what was here on Earth was less important to believers than what was to be found in heaven.

These two ideas, understood in different ways over time and combined with later events in Europe, like the **Enlightenment** and the **Industrial Revolution**, led to a shift in values that put people at the center. It allowed them to see nature as something to be used and exploited as they chose, and encouraged them to produce more, build more, want more and consume more, no matter the cost. Acquiring wealth and possessions became the cornerstone of European, now Western, culture.

SEPARATE AND SUPERIOR, OR ONE AMONG MANY?

The idea that humans are separate from and superior to nature, and that everything nonhuman exists only to be exploited by humans, is called anthropocentrism. It's easy to see how anthropocentrism—in religion, philosophy and science—would go on to fuel much of the harm that some human civilizations have done, both to other cultures and to the planet, through things like:

colonialism—a policy of taking control of a place and its people, in order to exploit its resources, by occupying it with *settlers*

capitalism—an economic system in which the goal is to make as much profit as possible for businesses and their owners

globalization—the growing interdependence of the world's economies, cultures and populations

These ways of thinking about our place in the order of things have given us permission to destroy, sometimes overnight, ecosystems that have taken millions of years to evolve.

The opposite of anthropocentrism is biocentrism, which sees humans as just one species among many, and nonhuman things as having value in and of themselves, not just as resources for humans to exploit. Many people believe that in order to begin to heal the earth—and ourselves—we all need to be *biocentric*. That's a big challenge! But doing whatever each of us can to restore the places where we live, work and play is a great start.

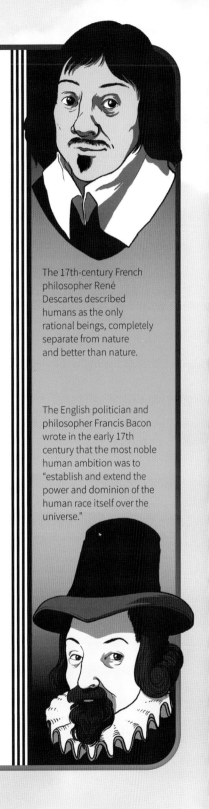

The 17th-century French philosopher René Descartes described humans as the only rational beings, completely separate from nature and better than nature.

The English politician and philosopher Francis Bacon wrote in the early 17th century that the most noble human ambition was to "establish and extend the power and dominion of the human race itself over the universe."

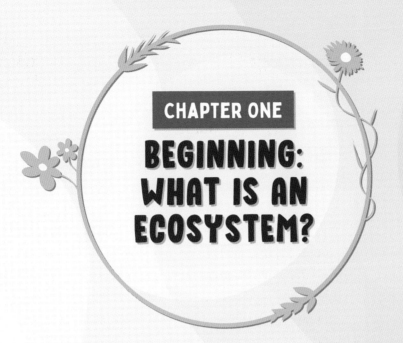

CHAPTER ONE

BEGINNING: WHAT IS AN ECOSYSTEM?

So what do we mean when we talk about ecosystems? In this chapter, we're going to find out by looking at nature through the eyes of an *ecologist*, someone who studies the relationships between living things, including humans, and their environment.

IT'S ALL ABOUT CONNECTION

An ecosystem is made up of a group of living things—whether on land, in water or in the air—that are connected in different ways with each other and with the nonliving parts of their environment, such as water, oxygen and sunlight. Or we can look at it another way and say that every *organism*—a living thing, such as a plant, animal, insect, fish, fungus, virus or bacterium—exists in a set of *relationships* that together form an ecosystem.

Sea stars, sea anemones, sea urchins and barnacles—colorful and diverse life in a tide-pool ecosystem.
DARILYNN/SHUTTERSTOCK.COM

IFISH/GETTY IMAGES

WILD IDEA

Ecology, the study of the relationships between living things and their environment, comes from the ancient Greek words *oikos*, meaning "house" or "dwelling place," and *logia*, meaning "study of."

Each organism in an ecosystem does what it needs to do to survive, such as getting food, water and shelter and reproducing. Since everything in an ecosystem is connected, what one organism does affects everything else in the system. Removing or adding a species, for example, will affect everything else, for better or worse.

An ecosystem can be as small as the community of creatures living in a tidal pool or as large as the oceans—or, largest of all, Earth itself. But even the smallest ecosystems are so complex that it's almost impossible to map out all the ways in which the living and nonliving parts interact. And since they are also constantly adapting to other factors, like weather, or events like fire and floods, they are always changing. They never stand still. In other words, ecosystems are dynamic.

66 **WHEN WE TRY TO PICK OUT ANYTHING BY ITSELF, WE FIND IT HITCHED TO EVERYTHING ELSE IN THE UNIVERSE.** **99** • JOHN MUIR

ECOSYSTEM SERVICES: WE CAN'T LIVE WITHOUT THEM

As just one of the millions of species of organisms on the planet, humans depend on other living and nonliving things to survive. In the 1970s ecologists began to think about exactly *how* we benefit from ecosystems. They called these benefits *ecosystem services*, and they can actually be given dollar values.

There are four types of ecosystem services:

PROVISIONING SERVICES give us our food in the form of grains, vegetables, fruit and meat from the land, and fish from lakes and oceans. We also get water to drink, wood for building and heating, plants for making medicines, clothes and other materials, and minerals for making tools and other things.

CULTURAL SERVICES are the benefits we get from nature just by being in or near it. Green spaces where we can play, exercise and relax benefit our physical and mental health—our bodies and minds. Natural places support different kinds of tourism, which not only contributes to local economies but can also help educate people about environmental issues. Nature inspires our art, culture and science and plays an important role in traditional knowledge, spirituality and religion. Nature provides a sense of place and belonging.

REGULATING SERVICES help keep the planet livable. For example, trees and other plants filter air and water and hold soil in place to prevent *erosion*, flooding and storm damage. Bees and other insects pollinate our food crops. Microorganisms in soil and wetlands break down our waste. And forests, soil and oceans absorb and store carbon from the atmosphere, which is especially important in relation to climate change.

WILD IDEA

A habitat is a place or environment that provides all of the things an organism needs to survive and reproduce: food, water, shelter and space. Since an ecosystem consists of all of the relationships of the organisms within it, it will also include all of those organisms' habitats.

4 **SUPPORTING SERVICES** are the processes that allow the earth to sustain not just people and ecosystems but life itself. They include:

- photosynthesis—the use of sunlight, water and carbon dioxide by plants to create oxygen and energy
- nutrient cycling—the movement of the elements we need to survive, including carbon, nitrogen and oxygen, between living things, the earth and the atmosphere
- the water cycle—the endless process that connects all of the water on the earth

Without supporting services, none of the other ecosystem services would be possible.

ECOSYSTEMS OF ALL STRIPES

There are many different types of ecosystems and different ways of classifying or naming them, but the three main types are **TERRESTRIAL, FRESHWATER** and **OCEAN**.

> **TERRESTRIAL ECOSYSTEMS** exist on land. The specific type of terrestrial ecosystem in a place—whether it's a forest or a rainforest, a grassland or a desert— depends on how hot and cold it gets, how much rain or snow falls, and how much light the area receives.

> **FRESHWATER ECOSYSTEMS** are found in lakes, rivers, ponds and wetlands, which have water that isn't salty and can be used for drinking and agriculture.

HOW MUCH IS AN ECOSYSTEM SERVICE WORTH?

Giving ecosystem services a concrete value is a good way to show people, businesses and governments the real importance of ecosystems. Scientists estimate that the world's ecosystems contribute more than US$125 trillion to the global *economy* every year. Not understanding this value allows humans to degrade the environment without thinking about the consequences.

» **OCEAN (OR MARINE) ECOSYSTEMS** include, in addition to the oceans themselves, *estuaries*, coral reefs and coastal areas. Ocean ecosystems cover almost 70 percent of Earth's surface. The organisms that live in these ecosystems must be able to survive in salt water.

The UN Decade on Ecosystem Restoration breaks these three main ecosystem types into eight categories:

- » forests
- » oceans and coasts
- » grasslands, shrublands and savannas
- » farmlands
- » freshwaters
- » peatlands
- » urban areas
- » mountains

You will see profiles of the UN ecosystem categories scattered throughout this book.

UNITED NATIONS ECOSYSTEM CATEGORY
FORESTS

There are many types of forests, including:

- temperate deciduous forests, like the boreal forest that encircles the earth
- tropical rainforests, like those of the Amazon
- urban forests, the trees in towns and cities

Together they provide habitat for much of the world's *biodiversity*. They store vast amounts of carbon, helping to moderate the climate. And for us humans, forests provide food, shelter, energy, medicines and jobs. Urban forests also provide shade, helping keep cities cool.

Challenges

- Continuing loss of forest—for example, 11.6 million acres (4.7 million hectares) of tropical rainforest are still lost each year, mostly to make way for new agricultural areas producing palm oil and beef
- Remaining forests degraded by logging and firewood cutting and further weakened by drought and by pests and diseases accidentally introduced from other parts of the world
- Intense forest fires fueled by climate change, destroying forest ecosystems

Actions We Can Take

- Plant trees.
- Protect or reintroduce native plants and animals.
- Protect water, soil and other parts of ecosystems so the trees we plant will grow.

These actions are being taken on a small scale—for example, on farms and in other rural areas, as well as in urban parks and backyards. They can also be taken on a very large scale, involving entire countries or continents.

Workers protecting "General Sherman," a 2,200 year-old redwood in California, the largest tree in the world, from an approaching wildfire.
ELIZABETH WU, NPS PHOTO

DISTURBANCE: GOOD OR BAD?

It's easy to imagine the earth as a giant machine with its countless parts working together, from the most minuscule ecosystems to the largest, in perfect harmony. While that's a lovely idea, it would mean that ecosystems were always the same, or static. In reality, since the very first life appeared on the earth about 3.7 billion years ago, in the form of microorganisms

like bacteria and algae, the only thing that has stayed the same has been change! Every ecosystem exists in a state of change, whether slow or fast.

One of the sources of change in ecosystems is **disturbance**, an event or force that affects their living and sometimes nonliving parts. Natural disturbances include fires, floods, windstorms, diseases and even volcanoes. Human-caused disturbances include things like damming of rivers, clearing of land for farming or urban

RESTORATION SNAPSHOT
10 BILLION TREE TSUNAMI

Pakistan has the fifth-largest population in the world—in a land area that is only the 33rd-largest in size (about twice the size of California). The climate crisis is affecting the country in many ways, including higher temperatures, melting glaciers in the Himalayan Mountains, heavier monsoon rains and more extreme droughts. People who live in poverty are hit hardest by these changes. So for Pakistan, where almost a quarter of the population lives in poverty, these effects are especially intense. Deforestation, caused by people in poverty burning wood for fuel and by wealthier people and criminals cutting trees for timber, has added to the effects of the climate crisis.

FIX

One province in Pakistan started a tree-planting project in 2015, nicknamed the Billion Tree Tsunami. It was so successful that a national program, the 10 Billion Tree Tsunami, began in 2019, with the goal of planting 10 billion trees across the country by 2023. Hundreds of thousands of people planted and took care of 21 different tree species, including the country's official national tree, the deodar. Others worked to protect the remaining forests so trees could regenerate naturally and survive.

The island of Borneo is a biodiversity hotspot. But between 2000 and 2018, more than 15 million acres (6 million hectares) of rainforest was logged, and most of it was then converted to palm oil plantations. Important habitat for endangered plants and animals, including Bornean elephants and orangutans and the critically endangered Sumatran rhinoceros, has been lost. Huge amounts of carbon are released into the atmosphere when forests like these are destroyed, contributing to climate change.

FIX

In the last 20 years, the Borneo Rainforest Rehabilitation Project has protected 62,000 acres (25,000 hectares) from more logging and degradation. It is also restoring nearly half of that, planting trees from a new nursery that can grow one million seedlings per year and helping native trees and vegetation regenerate on their own so that wildlife can return. The project also trains and employs local people.

RESTORATION SNAPSHOT
BORNEO RAINFOREST REHABILITATION PROJECT

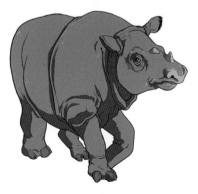

development, the introduction of new (*exotic*) and *invasive species*, and, more recently, pollution and climate change.

Disturbances either benefit or harm ecosystems, depending on how large and severe they are. For example, grasslands and some forests actually rely on regular local fires for renewal. But other disturbances, especially the human kind, can alter and even destroy ecosystems. Fortunately, as you'll see in the next chapters, we're learning how to undo some of that damage.

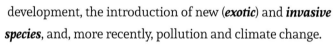

EVERYTHING DEPENDS ON KEYSTONE SPECIES

Every ecosystem has certain species that have a large effect on the system as a whole and on all the other species in it, which the ecosystem relies on for balance. A *keystone species* might be a large predator, like a wolf, which keeps the populations of other animals in check, or a large plant, like the saguaro cactus in the Sonoran Desert, which provides food and shelter for several animals. But other organisms, like fungi, bacteria and even hummingbirds (which act as pollinators, along with bees and other insects) can also be keystone species—the glue that holds the ecosystem together.

When a keystone species is removed from an ecosystem—whether through overhunting, overharvesting, disease or some other problem—many other species will be affected, and the ecosystem's biodiversity may be lost. On the other hand, protecting a keystone species can help protect the entire ecosystem, and reintroducing a keystone species can sometimes help restore the ecosystem.

The saguaro cactus is a keystone species in the Sonoran Desert, providing food for insects, bats, birds and mammals, as well as important nesting and perching sites for birds.
PATRICK JENNINGS/SHUTTERSTOCK.COM

UNITED NATIONS ECOSYSTEM CATEGORY
GRASSLANDS, SHRUBLANDS AND SAVANNAS

Drylands are areas without much water. They are found on every continent except Antarctica and cover more than 41 percent of the earth's land surface, including 77 percent of Australia and 66 percent of Africa. Drylands include deserts, of course, but also three other important ecosystems:

- grasslands—large areas dominated by grasses
- shrublands—areas dominated by shrubs and bushes
- savannas—grassland areas with scattered trees

Even without much water, these ecosystems can support large amounts of biodiversity. In fact, many of the world's **biodiversity hotspots** are found in them. Drylands also store a lot of carbon, helping to regulate climate. And in many places they are used for livestock grazing, providing both food and livelihoods for almost two billion people.

Grasslands that were once rich in biodiversity, converted to a monoculture of wheat.

LOURENCOLF/SHUTTERSTOCK.COM

WILD IDEA

Of the 8.7 million species that scientists have estimated to exist on Earth, only 1.2 million have been identified so far. That means millions of other species are still to be discovered. Scientists think there are at least 1 trillion species—and maybe more—if you include all the microorganisms, such as bacteria, on the planet. That's more than the estimated number of stars that make up the Milky Way!

Challenges

- About 70 percent of the world's grasslands and 50 percent of its savannas converted for growing crops and grazing livestock
- Erosion and loss of soil through poor agricultural practices like growing **monocultures** (growing only one crop over large areas and for a long time) and overgrazing by livestock
- Loss of native plant and animal species, and rapid spread of invasive species

Actions We Can Take

- Stop converting grasslands and savannas for agriculture.
- Protect grasslands, shrublands and savannas from further degradation.

- Reintroduce native plants and animals and take care of them until they have matured.
- Work closely with the people who depend on these ecosystems for their livelihoods, to make sure they benefit from restoration as well.

Tallgrass prairie, a type of grassland, in Nebraska.

CHERYL A. MEYER/SHUTTERSTOCK.COM

RESTORATION SNAPSHOT
REGREENING AFRICA

In sub-Saharan Africa (all the countries south of the Sahara Desert), 83 percent of people depend on land for their livelihoods. But about two-thirds of that land has been degraded by increased agriculture to feed the growing population. The result is less ***food security*** and more poverty, and the climate crisis is adding to these problems.

FIX

Agroforestry—planting trees on land used for food crops and livestock grazing—has already helped restore the land in several places in Africa. Good agroforestry practices can improve the soil, prevent erosion, create shade, slow strong winds, increase carbon storage both above and below the ground and provide fuel, food, fiber, medicines and more. Regreening Africa is a project that aims to have 500,000 households sustainably managing 2.5 million acres (1 million hectares) of land in eight countries across the continent (Ethiopia, Ghana, Kenya, Mali, Niger, Rwanda, Senegal and Somalia), using the agroforestry practices that suit them best. This will reduce poverty, increase food security and resilience to climate change and restore ecosystems, increasing ecosystem services as well.

Think ABOUT THIS

WHY IS BIODIVERSITY SUCH A BIG DEAL?

Biodiversity (short for "biological diversity") refers to the variety—or the *amount* of variety—among living things on Earth. This includes everything from the differences within a single species (for example, differences between the genes of a particular plant species that result in different sizes, shapes and colors) to the range of species within an ecosystem to the richness of species on the entire planet. And it's part of what makes the earth so astonishing and beautiful.

But as the population of humans has grown over the last few centuries, and we have damaged or altered ecosystems across the planet, biodiversity has come under increasing threat. Two-thirds of the world's population of wild animals has been lost in the last 50 years. And one million species are now facing extinction and could be lost forever. Why does the loss of biodiversity matter? Because if too many parts of an ecosystem are removed, the ecosystem can no longer function. And then we no longer benefit from its services. Losing a lot of ecosystem services will threaten all life on Earth.

The biologists Paul and Anne Ehrlich have compared this to the wing of an airplane. You can remove a few of the screws that hold it together and still fly safely. But if you keep removing them, at some point the wing will fall apart and the plane will no longer fly.

According to the World Wildlife Fund, the five main threats to biodiversity are:

- destroying ecosystems like rainforests and grasslands for human uses like agriculture and urban development

- pollution

- overharvesting

- climate change

- invasive species and disease

The good news is that we can reduce all of these threats if we try. Read on!

BIODIVERSITY HOTSPOTS

A biodiversity hotspot is a region with two special characteristics. First, it has a large number of plant species that grow nowhere else in the world. Second, those plants are under threat from things like development, pollution and disease. Scientists have listed 36 biodiversity hotspots around the world, including places like the tropical grasslands of the Cerrado in Brazil, the coastal forests of Eastern Africa and the Himalayas in Asia. The hotspots cover only about 2.5 percent of the planet's surface but support more than half of the plant species and 43 percent of the bird, mammal, amphibian and reptile species that exist nowhere else. Losing any of those species means they're gone forever. But conserving those areas will also save a lot of our biodiversity.

CHAPTER TWO

RESTORING

With our rapidly growing population over the last few centuries, we humans have made quite a mess of things on this beautiful blue planet. Can we fix the ecosystems we've damaged? Fortunately, we have lots of options.

> ❝ **IT'S KNOWING WHAT CAN BE DONE THAT GIVES PEOPLE THE COURAGE TO FIGHT.** ❞ • JANE GOODALL

CONSERVING WHAT'S LEFT

First, we need to protect the biodiversity that we still have, and all the ecosystems that support it, and prevent further damage from being done. This is called *conservation*. It may seem like a tall order, but it's happening! Large international organizations like the World Wildlife Fund and

Young volunteers planting native grass seedlings.
SCOTT SHARAGA/NPS PHOTO

WILD IDEA

Conservation biology is the science that supports conservation activities. It aims to understand biodiversity in all its forms, investigate the impacts of humans on species and ecosystems and find ways to protect them.

the International Union for Conservation of Nature have conservation projects all over the world, often focusing on protecting specific species and their habitats. Some organizations focus on a single species or group of species, like the Jane Goodall Institute, which protects gorillas and chimpanzees and their habitats, and Panthera, which protects the world's 40 species of wildcats.

RESTORING WHAT'S DAMAGED

In addition to protecting nature, we also need to undo some of the damage that's been done. This is the job of *ecological restoration*—assisting the recovery of an ecosystem that has been degraded, damaged or destroyed—and the focus of the United Nations Decade on Ecosystem Restoration. That word *assisting* in the definition of ecological restoration is important. It means that we aren't simply rebuilding an ecosystem part by part—which probably wouldn't be possible anyway because of the incredible complexity of ecosystems—but we are helping the ecosystem repair itself. This might mean removing the things that are causing the damage, like sources of pollution. Or allowing processes that people have prevented, like fire, to happen again. Or putting back certain plants,

ALDO LEOPOLD'S EXPERIMENT

One of the earliest restoration projects was an experiment conducted by the American ecologist, philosopher, writer and teacher Aldo Leopold. In 1935 he bought an old farm near the University of Wisconsin, where he worked, and every weekend he and his family planted trees and native plants in an effort to recreate the original prairie, which had been converted to cornfields. He would drive around Wisconsin looking for native grasses and wildflowers, like compass plant, dig them up or gather their seeds and then plant them on his patch of prairie. Leopold wrote about what he learned in his most famous book, *A Sand County Almanac*, which was published in 1949, a year after his death. It describes one of his best-known ideas, the land ethic (you'll read more about that in chapter 4).

animals and other organisms that have been removed and then carefully watching what happens.

The ideal restoration would result in an ecosystem perfectly restored to the way it was at a specific point in history. But that's usually not possible. Even with a lot of human help, ecosystems can't always return to the way they were just before they were affected by human activities. We can't always know exactly what an ecosystem was like at a certain point in time, since ecosystems are always changing. The type of ecosystem and how damaged it is, how well the restoration project is planned and done, and sometimes the amount of money available, will all help determine what happens. But most often, key parts of an ecosystem, such as its main species, and some of the ways the ecosystem functions, can be restored so that it continues to provide at least some of the ecosystem services it once did.

WILD IDEA

Restoration ecology is the science that supports the practice of ecological restoration. Like conservation biology, it relies on knowledge from many different sciences. But while conservation biology often aims to protect and increase the population of a certain species, restoration ecology focuses on rebuilding ecosystems that contain many species.

A father and son work with other volunteers in Thailand, planting a mix of mangrove trees and shrubs. Restoring mangroves reduces erosion and protects the coastline, increases carbon storage and provides habitat for organisms in and above the water.

MANIT LARPLUECHAI/DREAMSTIME.COM

SO HOW *DO* YOU RESTORE AN ECOSYSTEM?

As we saw in chapter 1, ecosystems are extremely complex things. Restoring damaged ecosystems can be complicated as well, depending on the type of ecosystem, where and how big it is and how badly damaged it is. But no matter its size, every restoration project involves a series of important steps.

1. PLANNING

As with any kind of project, a restoration project needs a lot of planning. Whether it's large or small, and no matter what kind of ecosystem is to be restored, the first step in planning is to find out who the stakeholders are. These are the people who might be affected by the project, such as Indigenous people, neighbors, farmers, hunters, fishermen, scientists, government agencies and/or businesses. The bigger the project, the more stakeholders there might be. They all need to be involved, to resolve any conflicts between their needs, use their knowledge and set goals everyone can agree on.

Planning also includes finding out as much as possible about the ecosystem, including its history and how or why it was damaged. Say a wetland was drained 20 years ago. There will be people who remember what it was like, and there might be lots of photos or other records to look at. In those cases it will be fairly easy to understand what the restored wetland should be like. But sometimes, as is often the case with forests or grasslands cleared for farming, the damage has been done over a long time, even centuries, and the ecosystem can be harder to understand. Once the planners know what it used to be like, they have to decide whether it's possible to fully restore the ecosystem, so that it eventually returns to its original state, or whether only some parts of it can be restored. If it can only be partly restored, what will that look like exactly?

2. DOING THE WORK

Next the planners decide *how* to restore the ecosystem. The methods they choose will depend on the type of ecosystem, its size and location, what needs to be done and the goals the stakeholders have agreed upon for the project. It will also depend on how much money is available for the project. Restoring a grassland area might include first removing invasive plants—by pulling them out by hand or with machines, or by using fire or chemical pesticides. Restoration on an island might involve removing invasive animals like rats, which eat seabird eggs, or goats, which eat plants. (In some places, though, goats can be used to remove invasive plants!) Many restoration projects will also involve reintroducing **native species**—the plants, animals and other organisms that were once there.

Larger restoration projects might have to begin with removing big structures like dams or old factories. The path

An excavator manually recreating the natural curves in a river.
SMEREKA/SHUTTERSTOCK.COM

of a river that was straightened might have to be recreated with its original curves. Or healthy soil, compost or rocks need to be added. Some temporary structures might have to be built—to keep water flowing where it needs to, for example, or to prevent erosion. Work like this obviously must be done with large machines and many different kinds of experts, from engineers to biologists. Once the heavy work is done, native plants and animals can be reintroduced, sometimes in a gradual process over many years.

3. MONITORING

Just as important as the earlier steps is keeping an eye on what happens in the restored ecosystem once the actual work is done to make sure that everything is working as hoped for and the goals for the restoration are being achieved. This is called monitoring. Are the plants and animals that were introduced surviving, and are other native species returning on their own? Are invasive species returning? And if they are, how should they be dealt with? Is water flowing where it's supposed to, and is there enough of it? Are new structures that were built doing what they're supposed to do?

4. LEARNING

Since ecosystems are so complex, and many of the factors that influence them, like weather, can't be controlled, things might not go exactly as planned. Further work might have to be done to keep the project on track. In fact, many restored ecosystems will need some help for a long time, even forever, to prevent them from falling back to their damaged state. There will likely be many lessons learned along the way, which can be used both in the project as it continues and in future restoration projects.

PLANNING

LEARNING

The steps in a restoration project are actually part of an ongoing cycle, moving from planning to working to monitoring to learning, then starting again. Everything learned in the first cycle affects how each step in the next cycle is done, over and over again until the project is finished.

DOING

MONITORING

Volunteers learn to plant grasses and other plants to restore the sand dunes on the beaches of Australia's Gold Coast. Without the dunes, the sandy beaches and the organisms they support wash away.

CHAMELEONSEYE/SHUTTERSTOCK.COM

NOVEL ECOSYSTEMS: GOOD OR BAD?

Several years ago ecologists began to talk about a new kind of ecosystem—the novel (new) ecosystem. Novel ecosystems are usually the result of human activities. They are made up of both native and exotic or invasive species, which have adapted to each other and created their own balance. They don't need any human help to survive, and the ecosystem can't be returned to its past natural state through restoration. Examples of novel ecosystems are forests that have been completely taken over by an invasive plant, like kudzu in the southern United States, or abandoned agricultural fields that have been damaged by chemical fertilizers and other forms of pollution.

The problem with many novel ecosystems is that they support less biodiversity than the original ecosystem did. Most plants and animals have evolved to rely on very specific conditions, including food, water, shelter and light. When exotic or invasive species move into an ecosystem, many of these conditions change, so the native species can no longer survive there. Novel ecosystems may also provide fewer ecosystem services because they no longer function the way they used to.

The idea of novel ecosystems has created a lot of controversy. Some ecologists argue that it provides an excuse to stop protecting other ecosystems from harm and not bother trying to restore damaged ecosystems. They think people will just want to "manage" ecosystems so they work better for humans.

Others believe that we need to work with *all* of these options: protect remaining ecosystems, restore damaged ecosystems wherever we can *and* work with novel ecosystems to make them better. What do you think?

In chapter 3 we'll look at another controversial idea: rewilding.

UNITED NATIONS ECOSYSTEM CATEGORY
OCEANS AND COASTS

Oceans cover about 70 percent of the earth's surface. This United Nations ecosystem category includes oceans, coral reefs, coastal areas and estuaries. They store even more carbon than forests, regulate the planet's climate and host a great deal of its biodiversity. They also produce most of the oxygen we breathe, feed us, support our economies by providing jobs and protect us from floods.

KOSHKINA TATIANA/SHUTTERSTOCK.COM

HELPING MANGROVES REPAIR THEMSELVES

Mangroves, which grow on tropical and subtropical coasts around the world, provide important habitat for organisms both above and below the surface of the water—fish, shellfish, birds, reptiles and more. They store four times more carbon than rainforests. They also protect coastlines from erosion, flooding and storms. But we've lost more than 35 percent of the world's mangroves since 1980, many deforested for fuel and timber or cleared for buildings and agriculture.

FIX

Robin Lewis was a wetland scientist who has helped restore mangroves in 30 places in the United States and in 25 other countries around the world. Many mangrove restoration projects in the 1980s and 1990s failed, because people were planting a single type of seedling rather than many different kinds, as you would in a forest. They were also planting seedlings as you would on land, only to have them washed away by the rising and falling tides. Lewis figured out that if he created the right conditions, the mangroves would restore themselves. The creation of a slight slope through the use of machines allowed mangrove seeds arriving in the water from healthy mangroves nearby to take root and grow. It's hard work to get the conditions right, but when they *are* right, the mangroves quickly repair themselves.

Challenges

- Vast amounts of garbage (especially plastics), untreated sewage and chemicals dumped into the oceans
- Overfishing
- *Mangroves* (trees and shrubs that grow in salt water on the coasts of tropical and subtropical countries) removed
- Coral reefs and the many species they support damaged by climate change

Actions We Can Take

- Stop the flow of garbage and other pollutants into the oceans.
- Stop overfishing.
- Protect coral reefs, mangroves and estuaries from both human activities and the effects of climate change.

UNITED NATIONS ECOSYSTEM CATEGORY
FRESHWATERS

Freshwater ecosystems include lakes, rivers, streams, ponds and wetlands. We rely on them for water, food, energy and transportation. They provide habitat for countless species, store huge amounts of carbon, filter water and help prevent floods and droughts.

Challenges

- Overfishing
- Overuse of water for irrigation and industry
- Chemicals, sewage and garbage dumped into lakes and rivers
- Rivers dammed and turned into canals—only a third of the world's rivers still flow the way they did in the past
- Wetlands drained to create more agricultural land— we've lost 80 percent of the world's wetlands in the last 300 years
- One in three freshwater species facing extinction

ELENA11/SHUTTERSTOCK.COM

Actions We Can Take

- Stop polluting.
- Remove or redesign dams.
- Control our uses of water and the lands next to fresh-water ecosystems.
- Remove invasive species and restore native species.

RESTORATION SNAPSHOT
PLANTING SEAGRASS MEADOWS IN VIRGINIA

Seagrass meadows made up of more than 70 species of seagrass are found in the coastal waters of 159 countries, covering more than 116,00 square miles (300,000 square kilometers) around the world. They provide habitat for many marine species, protect coasts by holding the seabed in place with their roots and store large amounts of carbon—twice as much as forests on land. But seagrass meadows around the world have been damaged, often by pollution and bad fishing practices, and they are often unable to recover without help.

FIX

Over the last 20 years, scientists and volunteers have "planted" more than 70 million seagrass seeds, taken from a healthy meadow, in 500 acres (200 hectares) of Virginia seaside where disease and then a hurricane had destroyed the seagrass meadows. The 500 acres has already grown to nearly 10,000 acres (4,000 hectares)—improving water quality and bringing back marine species, including anchovies and blue crabs, that had been missing in the area for decades. Even the scientists are surprised by how quickly the meadows have bounced back! The project is now a model for restoring seagrass meadows around the world.

RESTORATION SNAPSHOT
REFLOWING THE KISSIMMEE RIVER

The Kissimmee River once wandered for 103 miles (166 kilometers) through the middle of Florida. It had a very wide floodplain (a flat area around a river that is regularly flooded) that provided habitat for many native wetland plants, birds and fish. But people living in the area didn't like the flooding, so in 1948 the government allowed the river to be widened, deepened and straightened. Work continued in the 1960s with the building of a deep canal, 38 miles (61 kilometers) long, extending straight through the river's winding path. While the flooding was reduced, much of the rich wetland ecosystem was destroyed, along with habitat supporting hundreds of species, some of them threatened or endangered.

FIX
In 1999 the world's largest river-restoration project at the time began with 8 miles (13 kilometers) of the canal being filled in. Today water has returned to about 44 miles (71 kilometers) of the original river channel, restoring about 44 square miles (114 square kilometers) of floodplain and habitat for returning native species.

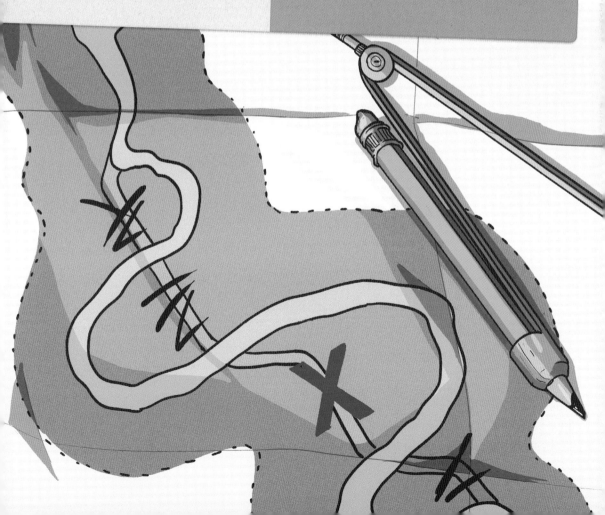

WHAT'S WITH ALL THESE *RE-* WORDS? (AND OTHER QUESTIONS ABOUT LANGUAGE)

Language is always complex, and words can gain many different meanings, even opposite meanings, as they evolve over time. When we're talking about complicated things, it's always useful to look carefully at the words we're using to see what they actually mean. For example, you might have noticed that there are a lot of verbs (action words) in this book that begin with *re-*. In English, the prefix *re-* has two meanings. The first is "again," as in redo (do it again), regenerate (generate again), rebuild (build again) and reintroduce (introduce again). The second is "back," as in return (go back or give back) and restore (put back or give back). In some words, like *rewild*, *re-* can actually mean both "again" and "back." (See how many *re-* verbs you can spot!)

But there are interesting questions lurking in the words *restore* and *rewild*—at least from an ecologist's point of view. Can ecosystems really be restored to the way they were before they were degraded? First there is the problem of deciding what point in history we want to return to. Ten years ago? A hundred years ago? Ten thousand years ago? And do we know enough about what the ecosystem was like at that time? Even if those issues can be resolved, there are more questions. If an ecosystem has been damaged to the point where it can't be fully repaired, by restoring it are we actually going back in time or forward to something entirely new? So many conditions are changing with the climate, maybe *everything* is going to be new and different. So many questions and not many answers!

WHAT DO WE MEAN BY *NATURE*?

Another word that pops up a lot in this book is *nature.* What comes into your mind when you think of nature? Maybe you see a forest, a flat or rolling prairie or snow-capped mountains. Maybe a quiet lake, a surging river or ocean waves crashing on a beach. Or maybe you think of a polar bear, a soaring eagle or some brightly colored fish darting about in an aquarium. If you live in a large city, you might think of nature as a leafy park or the noisy birds that crowd around a feeder full of sunflower seeds. Nature can mean many different things to different people.

As we've seen, while Western culture thinks of itself as separate from nature, some cultures think of nature simply as something they exist within. Some languages don't even have a word for nature, because the people who speak them don't think of nature as a "thing." But quite apart from that, *nature* is a complex word, with many different meanings. (The *Merriam-Webster Unabridged Dictionary* offers 15 different definitions!) And if the meaning of nature differs for different people and cultures, the idea of protecting it can become complicated as well. What, exactly, are we protecting? Are we protecting nature's resources for our own use? Are we protecting special things and landscapes—like the geysers in Yellowstone National Park or the Rocky Mountains in Banff National Park? Or are we protecting ourselves?

ER, WILDERNESS OR WILDNESS?

If all these questions aren't enough to make you want to go and solve some math problems instead, here's one more interesting word-related challenge. What do we mean by *wilderness*? What comes to your mind when you think of wilderness might depend on where you live and the places you've visited or read about. Again, in English it's a complicated word that has evolved from one meaning to another over centuries. But today it usually means a place of pristine nature unaffected by human activity, something to be preserved and protected, to be looked at from afar or to be experienced from within, usually for recreation.

It's amazing what two little letters can do. If we take the *er* out of *wilderness* we have *wildness*, which is a different thing altogether but also challenging to define. Some ecologists define it as "the basic ability of anything living to renew itself." (There's that *re-* prefix again!) In that sense, we can all do with a little wildness. But wildness is especially important for rewilding, which we're going to look at next.

CHAPTER THREE
REWILDING

Planning for ecological restoration has always included deciding what state to return an ecosystem to. For example, if you were restoring an area of prairie or grassland, you might aim to return it to what it was like before it was plowed under for cornfields in 1900. Restoring a small river that European settlers dammed in 1850, your goal might be what the river was like before that, keeping in mind that the river might also have been used and modified by the Indigenous Peoples in the area long before that. But about 40 years ago, some biologists took this idea a little further…

GOING WAY, *WAY* BACK

Twelve thousand years further, to be exact. They argued that at the end of the Pleistocene epoch (what we often call the Ice Age, from about 2.6 million years ago to 12,000 years ago), when the very large animals (megafauna) of North and South

Reintroducing important predators, like these wolves, to a severely damaged ecosystem can help repair the ecosystem and restore its biodiversity.
JIMKRUGER/GETTY IMAGES

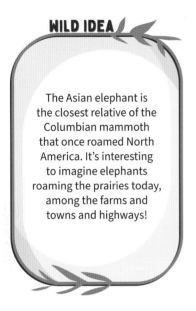

America, Australia, Europe and Asia went extinct, nothing took their place. No one knows for sure why the Pleistocene megafauna went extinct, but one possible explanation is that early humans, whose populations were growing and spreading, overhunted them.

The result was that the ecosystems the megafauna were an important part of were permanently damaged. **Food chains** (who eats whom, in sequence) and **food webs** (all the food chains in an ecosystem) were broken, and species that had evolved together were no longer together, which weakened the populations of some remaining species and exploded others.

LIONS AND TIGERS AND BEARS

This means that many of the ecosystems we think of as having been damaged since the Industrial Revolution and colonization were *already* weakened, which made them even more sensitive to human impacts. So the scientists argued further that reintroducing large animals similar to those that went extinct would solve certain ecological problems—for example, areas where deer no longer had natural predators now had very large populations that were damaging entire ecosystems. In North America, this would mean reintroducing the American bison to areas where it had long been absent, and maybe even introducing cheetahs, jaguars and African lions, which most closely resemble extinct species.

This idea, called **Pleistocene rewilding**, has been tried in various forms in Europe. Rewilding projects have introduced European bison, water buffalo, beavers, wild horses and cattle that resemble the aurochs, their extinct ancestor. Some scientists think Pleistocene rewilding doesn't make sense because ecosystems have

evolved so much in the thousands of years since the end of the Pleistocene. But there have been some exciting successes—along with a few failures.

WAIT—WHAT IS REWILDING, EXACTLY?

While Pleistocene rewilding may seem like a pretty wild idea, rewilding without the Pleistocene part has become very popular. It's also an idea that is changing quickly as the climate crisis becomes more urgent and needs a lot of different solutions.

Scientists and others who practice rewilding define it in many different ways, which can make it a little confusing. But generally rewilding means reintroducing missing megafauna to restore long-damaged food chains and the processes that made the ecosystem function properly. The goal of

Konik horses are the closest living relatives of the tarpan, the extinct wild horse of northern Europe. Wild konik horses were introduced in one of the earliest rewilding projects in Europe: the Oostvaardersplassen in the Netherlands.

rewilding is ecosystems that have recovered their wildness and biodiversity so they can be self-sustaining—meaning they can survive with little or no human help.

There are also different types of rewilding. Like Pleistocene rewilding, trophic rewilding focuses on reintroducing large animals at the top of the food chain in order to repair ecosystems and restore biodiversity, but without the extinct animals. Passive rewilding is used mostly in European farmlands that have been abandoned, letting them do what they will without any human involvement at all.

We don't yet know how well rewilding will work, especially in ecosystems near agricultural and urban areas. We may still have to deal with problems like invasive species, conflict between humans and wildlife (and between humans themselves) and disturbances like fires and floods so that the ecosystems benefit and humans aren't harmed. Time will tell…

WHAT IS THE DIFFERENCE BETWEEN REWILDING AND RESTORATION?

It can sometimes be hard to understand the difference between rewilding and restoration. But generally speaking, in rewilding people are less involved or less in control. Where a restoration project might reintroduce native species at some point, it likely will also include removing invasive species, sometimes for many years, and in some cases removing large structures, like dams and buildings, and changing other physical aspects of the ecosystem. People might have to "manage" the ecosystem for a long time, even forever, to keep it from collapsing. In a rewilding project, though, people might reintroduce one or more large animal species, and maybe not all at once, but then they will step back and watch whatever happens to the ecosystem. This means that rewilding can be much less expensive than ecological restoration.

Before (above) and after (below) the Elwa Dam, in Washington State, was removed.
NPS PHOTO

THE WOLVES OF YELLOWSTONE

One of the best-known examples of trophic rewilding, even though the term wasn't known at the time, happened in Yellowstone National Park. When the park was created in 1872, the wildlife within it wasn't protected the way it is today. European settlers in the area didn't like wolves because they competed for the same food sources, like deer and bison. Hungry wolves would also prey on settlers' livestock. Seen as a pest by settlers, the wolves were hunted down, and by about 1925 they no longer existed in Yellowstone.

The loss of the wolves led to an explosion in the elk population. The elk ate a lot of plants and young trees,

which affected birds and beavers. The loss of plants along riverbanks led to serious erosion, reducing the quality of the water, and the loss of shade increased water temperature, which in turn affected fish. The entire ecosystem of the park deteriorated.

As scientists began to understand more about ecosystems and the complex and interconnected relationships within them, people began to campaign for a return of wolves to Yellowstone. In 1995, 14 wolves were moved into the park from Canada, and another 17 were released in 1996. The effects on the ecosystem could soon be seen. The elk population shrank. Willows, poplars and other trees grew back along the rivers. The beaver population grew. Berry plants grew back, and the grizzly bear population grew. The coyote

STAN TEKIELA/GETTY IMAGES

population also shrank, which in turn increased the numbers of rabbits and mice, which then supported hawks, foxes and badgers. The ecosystem still hasn't returned to what it was before the wolves were removed, and it might never recover fully, but the story has taught scientists and others a lot about how nature works.

THE THREE C'S—THEN AND NOW

When the rewilding idea was first introduced in the 1980s, an important part of it was the Three C's: Cores, Corridors and Carnivores. Today the Three C's are Core areas, Connectivity and Coexistence.

1985 THREE C'S	TODAY'S THREE C'S
CORES: Areas where ecosystems are protected—over a very large area there might be several cores, consisting of wilderness areas, national parks or privately owned natural areas	**CORE AREAS:** Areas where ecosystems are protected
CORRIDORS: Areas that allow wildlife to move between cores	**CONNECTIVITY:** Healthy ecosystems running between the cores so species have larger areas to move through
CARNIVORES: Apex predators, reintroduced at the top of the food chain	**COEXISTENCE:** Natural or human-made barriers help ensure that wildlife and humans (and their livestock) can live near each other without too much conflict

WILD IDEA

Removing a large predator from an ecosystem, or adding one, causes large changes in the food chain, called a trophic cascade. For example, removing wolves from an ecosystem increases the number of deer or elk, which in turn decreases the populations of plants they eat and that other animals depend on.

BISON ON THE GREAT PLAINS

Another North American example of rewilding involves the American bison. Until the 19th century, tens of millions of bison roamed the Great Plains of the United States. As they fed mainly on grasses that would otherwise dominate, their eating habits allowed other types of plants to grow. The bison killed shrubs and trees by rubbing their bodies and horns on them, which kept the plains from becoming forest. They liked to wallow, rolling on the ground to shed loose fur and keep insects from biting, and this created dips in the ground where plant species other than those found on the plains could grow. They also moved constantly across the landscape, grazing in some places and not others, and pooping nutrients as they went.

All these activities helped support the amazing biodiversity of the Great Plains. Equally important, for Indigenous Peoples on the plains, such as the Niitsitapi, Lakota and Tsuut'ina nations, bison were an essential source of food, clothing, blankets and other materials, and the Peoples' ways of life depended on the bison.

A mountain of skulls from the millions of bison that were shot, either for money or pleasure, in the late 19th century in an effort to completely and permanently remove them from the Great Plains.

COURTESY OF THE BURTON HISTORICAL COLLECTION, DETROIT PUBLIC LIBRARY

Today bison once again roam in some areas—like this herd stopping traffic in Yellowstone National Park.

GUOQIANG XUE/DREAMSTIME.COM

But in the late 1800s, European settlers and the US government wiped out the bison in an effort to destroy both the ecosystem and the Indigenous Peoples who relied on it. Millions of bison were shot, sometimes for fun, sometimes for money, but mainly to deprive the Indigenous Peoples of one of their most important resources. By 1890 fewer than 1,000 bison remained—some wild in Yellowstone National Park and northern Alberta, others in zoos and on private ranches.

Thankfully, a campaign to save the bison was successful. The few remaining animals were bred, and by 1920 there were about 12,000 in captivity. The 1960s saw the beginning of a movement to restore the bison, the grasslands and the cultures of the Great Plains. By the early 2000s there were about half a million bison, most as livestock on ranches but some on Native American lands and in new conservation and restoration areas. The National Bison Association's Bison One Million project aims to build the population in North America to a million by 2025.

> **WILD IDEA**
>
> Just as a keystone species is essential to an ecosystem, a *cultural keystone species* is essential to the life of a community. Salmon is a cultural keystone species for the Coast Salish peoples of the Pacific Northwest, just as bison are a cultural keystone species for the Indigenous Peoples of the Great Plains.

INTO THE FUTURE

The climate crisis is affecting the way some scientists think about rewilding. With the planet's temperature rising so quickly, patterns of rainfall changing, and severe storms, droughts and other "weather events" increasing, rewilding to a past state in an ecosystem may no longer be possible. If many of the factors that help shape an ecosystem change, the ecosystem will change as well. This means that the focus of rewilding—and maybe of restoration too—may need to be on the future rather than the past. The aim will be to let nature create new and unique "future wildness" rather than trying to recreate the past.

> " **WE MUST REWILD THE WORLD.** " • SIR DAVID ATTENBOROUGH, *A LIFE ON OUR PLANET*

UNITED NATIONS ECOSYSTEM CATEGORY
FARMLANDS

Farmlands are "modified ecosystems," created through people's work on the land, in many cases over hundreds and even thousands of years. Now covering more than a third of the earth's surface, they produce food and other resources for humanity and livelihoods for at least two billion people. They also support countless other plant and animal species.

Challenges

- About 80 percent of the world's farmlands affected by lack of water, loss of nutrients and increased salt in the soil, soil erosion and other problems
- Depletion of soil through modern farming practices, including growing large monocultures, using

chemical fertilizers and pesticides and removing
trees and hedges in and around fields

- Overgrazing by livestock, contributing to the loss of
native species and the spread of invasive species

Knepp Castle Estate, in
England, was farmed
until 2001, when its
3,500 acres (1,400
hectares) of land no
longer grew enough for
the owners to be able to
earn a living.

FIX

Owners Charlie Burrell and Isabella Tree restored the river that runs through the
land and the wetlands fed by the river. They introduced several species of grazing
animals that resemble the animals that would have lived there thousands of years
ago—longhorn cattle, wild ponies, pigs and three species of deer. And then they
stood back and let natural processes run their course. What happened surprised
everyone. Populations of common wildlife species—birds, bats, insects, butterflies,
moths, reptiles and small mammals—grew rapidly. Even better, rare and endangered
species of birds and butterflies began to return to the land, and their numbers have
grown as well. A study of the ecosystem services provided on the estate showed that,
for example, much more carbon was being stored than had been when the land was
being farmed, and flood protection was much greater as well. Knepp has become
a model for other people who are interested in rewilding land that is no longer
productive for farming, as well as a place for people to learn and relax in nature.

Knepp Castle Estate has reintroduced white storks, which hadn't bred in England for centuries.

MELANIE HOBSON/DREAMSTIME.COM

These problems make it harder for farmers to grow food, and this in turn makes food more expensive, contributing to poverty and ***food insecurity*** (when people are unable to afford the healthy food they need).

Actions We Can Take

- Grow a variety of different crops in each field, instead of just one or two.
- Use natural fertilizers and pest control instead of chemicals.
- Plant native plants, shrubs and trees in and around fields.
- Graze livestock sustainably by having different kinds of animals and always rotating them from one area to another.
- Use land for both growing crops and grazing livestock.

UNITED NATIONS ECOSYSTEM CATEGORY
PEATLANDS

RUDMER ZWERVER/DREAMSTIME.COM

Peatlands are ecosystems that are waterlogged, keeping dead plants from breaking down, or decomposing, to form soil. Instead they form a spongy material called peat, which can be cut and used for fuel. Peatlands occur on every continent, helping to regulate water levels and prevent flooding and drought, and they often contain rare species. Although they cover only about 3 percent of the earth's surface, they store almost 30 percent of its soil carbon. In fact, they absorb and store more carbon than any other terrestrial ecosystem, which makes them extremely important in the fight to keep the earth from warming further.

Challenges

- Peatlands drained for agriculture, forestry, fuel and other uses
- Stored carbon released when peatlands drained
- Burning of peat and peatlands releases even more carbon, contributing to global emissions
- Surrounding freshwater polluted and plants and animals harmed by a chemical called nitrate when peatlands drained

Actions We Can Take

- Keep peat in the ground and keep it wet!
- Stop draining peatlands.
- Restore degraded peatlands wherever possible by managing water flows and reintroducing native plants.
- Promote alternative energy sources to reduce use of peat as fuel.

Peatlands burning in the tundra, removing the insulating layers of peat, grass and roots and speeding up the thawing of permafrost—versus what a healthy peatland looks like, as seen on the opposite page.

Think ABOUT THIS

WHO'S GOING TO PAY FOR ALL THIS?

Governments usually end up paying for ecological restoration, which means we all pay for it through our taxes. Sometimes corporations also pay for restoring damage they've caused, or they donate money to large and small organizations that do conservation, restoration and rewilding, as part of being good corporate citizens.

Ecological restoration isn't cheap. Large restoration projects can cost a lot of money. Plants and animals can be costly to grow or buy, expensive equipment may be needed, and professionals need to be paid for their work. Rewilding can cost less because it usually involves less work, though the animals that are reintroduced can still be costly.

But *not* restoring the world's ecosystems will cost us far more. Economists (people who study the economy—the way we produce, buy and sell goods and services) estimate that half of the world's economy depends on nature. If we don't restore ecosystems and they continue to be degraded, $10 trillion in the global economy could be lost by 2050. That's a lot—and it will mean increased poverty and food insecurity for many people, and a lower standard of living for others.

RESTORATION PAYS FOR ITSELF

But the good news is that every dollar governments spend on restoration and rewilding will create $30 in economic benefits. Restoration work creates jobs—but it also makes sure that the ecosystems farmers, ranchers, fishers and others depend on are healthy, so that they can continue to have their livelihoods. For example:

> Restoring coral reefs, mangroves and other ocean ecosystems will also restore the fisheries that people around the world depend on for food and income.

Ecosystem restoration on agricultural land will also improve food security for billions of people.

Agroforestry—a type of farming in which trees are grown together with crops and livestock (animals)—could increase food security for 1.3 billion people all on its own.

Restoring wetlands, rivers and forests will give people in both rural and urban areas around the world better access to cleaner water, improving their water security. It can also save billions of dollars in water-treatment costs for large cities. Healthier ecosystems also mean improved physical and mental health. For example, planting trees in cities not only reduces air pollution but also lowers summer temperatures and reduces the effects of heat waves. And whether in cities or in rural areas, being in healthy ecosystems makes us feel better in a number of ways (more about that in chapter 4). Better health is good for all of us, of course, but it also saves governments a lot of money. And while healthier ecosystems will help slow climate change, they will also be more resilient (better able to cope) in the face of climate change, which is a good thing in every way. No matter how you look at it, restoring ecosystems will more than pay for itself!

YET ANOTHER *RE-* WORD: REGENERATIVE AGRICULTURE

Regenerative agriculture is a way of farming that improves the soil rather than depleting it, as modern agriculture usually does. Plowing (or tilling) erodes soil and releases a lot of carbon into the atmosphere, which is a major cause of climate change. By disturbing the soil less, using a diversity of plants in different places and at different times, and carefully managing water use, regenerative farming creates healthier soils that grow healthier crops and pull lots of carbon out of the atmosphere and into the ground—a win for everyone!

CHAPTER FOUR
PEOPLING

So far we've talked about humans mainly as a species that depends on nature, has harmed nature and now needs to repair nature, through restoration or rewilding, in order to survive. But if we take a more biocentric view and see ourselves as *part* of nature, can repairing nature help make our lives, our communities and our societies better too?

BACK TO NATURE

Scientists believe our species, *Homo sapiens*, has been around for at least 300,000 years, and until very recently, we all lived in nature. Wherever we lived on Earth, we killed animals for food and fur, harvested plants for food and fiber, cut wood for fuel and for building shelter, used water for drinking and hygiene. We moved rocks, diverted streams, cleared fields. And for thousands of years, the ecosystems we lived in adapted and evolved right along with us. Just like every other

Can we bring nature back to our urban landscapes of concrete, steel and glass to make them better places for everyone?

VIEW APART/SHUTTERSTOCK.COM

species, we played a specific role in those ecosystems, and everything we did was part of and helped shape them.

With all the speed and noise and technologies of modern life, especially in urban areas, it's easy to forget that we evolved in nature—that nature is as much a part of us as we are of it. Humans have evolved over millions of years, and our brains and bodies can't evolve as quickly as the tools and technologies we've invented in the last few hundred years and the lifestyles that have resulted. We're still hardwired to be in nature.

LESS SCREEN, MORE GREEN

In 2005 the writer Richard Louv introduced the term *nature-deficit disorder*. He believed that spending too much time indoors—because we want to work or play with our various devices or there is nowhere to play outdoors or parents are worried about traffic or crime—can cause a lot of different

health problems, especially for kids. The earth has suffered too, because we are forgetting how to be in nature and how to take care of it. Louv's ideas sparked a movement to get kids and adults back outdoors.

Other researchers have since looked at this the other way around—that is, how our physical and mental health can improve from being in nature, including in green spaces in towns and cities. Just taking a walk, or even looking out a window at some trees, can help us pay attention and learn better in school, improve memory, reduce stress and make us feel happier. And all these things can improve our physical health as well.

RESTORING HABITAT, RESTORING CONFIDENCE

In 2004 Wendy Kotilla started a small program called Youth and Ecological Restoration on Vancouver Island, British Columbia. Young people aged 12 to 18, who may have trouble connecting with school, their community or jobs, get the chance to work one-on-one with ecologists and others in community organizations to restore watersheds. They help restore habitat, enhance salmon stocks and monitor watersheds—connecting with nature, learning about their local ecosystems and gaining confidence in themselves. More than 400 young people have done the program, and more than 164 local community groups are now connected with it.

FORCED OUT

For many people around the world, the disconnection from nature—and the resulting harm—is about much more than spending too much time inside. In North America, for example, European settlers and their governments forced Indigenous Peoples off their lands, making them live on tiny fragments of what was once their territory, called reserves in Canada and reservations in the United States. In many cases, the loss of their lands also meant the loss of their ways of life, including their cultures and often their languages as well. Together with government policies such as forcing Indigenous children to attend residential schools, the effects on individuals, communities and entire cultures have been devastating.

RGBSPACE/GETTY IMAGES

In 2013 a group of Cree youth walked almost 1,000 miles (1,600 kilometers) from Whapmagoostui, QC, to Ottawa. They wanted to bring the many issues they were facing at home to the Canadian government's attention.

Unfortunately, people around the world—especially Indigenous Peoples—continue to be forced from their land today by governments and corporations that want to exploit the land and its resources. The results are usually the same as in the past—losing their land means losing their way of life and their culture, often leading to poverty and a range of health and other problems. Losing a way of life doesn't mean starting to live like everyone else in the dominant society. It often means continuing to be excluded from, or marginalized by, that society, through laws, policies and practices that prevent them from having any power.

TARGETS FOR POLLUTION

To make matters worse, racialized people, those who are living in poverty and people in other marginalized communities face greater impacts from air and water pollution, climate change and other environmental problems, including the degraded ecosystems we've been talking about. This is not an accident.

It's the result of **environmental racism**—government rules and regulations, and decisions by corporations, that allow areas in which these people live, both rural and urban, to be targeted for polluting industries and for dumping or storing toxic waste. Environmental racism has many extremely negative impacts on the mental and physical health of people in these communities.

Environmental justice is one answer to environmental racism. The environmental justice movement, which began in the United States in the 1980s, is today an international movement to ensure that all people can live, work, play and learn in a healthy environment, regardless of race, color, nationality, income, gender or age. Environmental justice includes both economic and social justice, and it respects not only biodiversity but also human or cultural diversity. Achieving environmental justice is a big challenge. It means changing laws and policies at every level, from local to global, and ensuring that everyone has the right to a healthy environment and the right to be heard.

People marching for environmental and other types of justice in Detroit in 2015.
JIM WEST/ALAMY STOCK PHOTO

LEFT OUT

Western science grew out of the idea that humans are separate from nature, so it's not surprising that activities like ecological restoration and rewilding, which are based on Western science, have tended to focus on the plants and (nonhuman) animals in ecosystems, often leaving humans out of the picture. Restoration and rewilding projects have aimed to get all the right (nonhuman) species back in an ecosystem and working together based on what they think it might have looked like at some point in history.

But projects like these can and do fail, for many different reasons. Most often it's because they've left out something very important—people! People who have lived in and around the ecosystems for generations, and sometimes for thousands of years. People who depend on, care about and often know a lot about the ecosystems—Indigenous people, neighbors, farmers, ranchers, fishers, loggers. Kids too!

Scientists who are planning restoration and rewilding projects sometimes forget to ask the people who still use the ecosystem, or whose ancestors used it, what they know about the plants and animals in it. There may be some important things the scientists don't know about and that will affect the success of the project. As we'll see in the next section, there are different ways of knowing things, and scientific knowing is only one of them.

Restoration and rewilding projects that don't consider all of the people who have a relationship with an ecosystem can do more harm than good, contributing to environmental racism rather than environmental justice. Or, to look at it the other way around, good restoration and rewilding projects are as good for people as they are for ecosystems.

WILD IDEA

Indigenous Peoples account for less than 5 percent of the planet's human population, but they own, occupy or use at least 25 percent of its land area, and protect 80 percent of the world's remaining biodiversity.

CARING FOR PEOPLE, CARING FOR LAND

The American ecologist Aldo Leopold already understood this idea when he was doing one of the first restoration projects (see chapter 2 sidebar "Aldo Leopold's Experiment"). In his book *A Sand County Almanac*, published in 1949, Leopold introduced what he called a land ethic. Ethics require that all members of a community treat one another with respect so all members benefit. But Aldo thought of community as including not just humans but the land as well—by which he meant plants, animals, soil, water and all other parts of the earth! So a land ethic is a caring relationship between people and land, in which caring for people can't be separated from caring for land.

THOUSANDS OF YEARS' WORTH OF KNOWLEDGE

Indigenous people who have grown up and lived their lives in the place where generations of their ancestors lived have special knowledge about that place and the relationships of the living beings within it. This is called traditional ecological knowledge, or TEK. (Some people also call it Indigenous knowledge.) TEK and scientific ecological knowledge (sometimes called SEK for short) are both based on paying close attention to what happens in an ecosystem. But unlike scientific ecological knowledge, TEK has grown out of thousands of years of observation of, and experience with, the connections and patterns in environments, rather than the

WHO BENEFITS? WHO'S HARMED?

Restoration and rewilding projects can fail because organizers didn't consult with everyone who could be affected in some way by the project. While some people might benefit from restoration and rewilding projects, others might actually be harmed by them. This can create a lot of conflict between different groups or simply prevent people from caring or wanting to help, which can in turn affect the success of a project. Even more worrying, the people who will be harmed by the project may already have so little power that they can't speak out or take action, and their situation will only be further worsened.

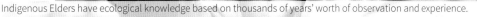

Indigenous Elders have ecological knowledge based on thousands of years' worth of observation and experience.
RUSLANA IURCHENKO/SHUTTERSTOCK.COM

few decades that scientists have been collecting data. TEK is also part of Indigenous cultures, woven right into the people's social and spiritual practices and beliefs.

> **" TO LOVE A PLACE "**
> **IS NOT ENOUGH.**
> **WE MUST FIND WAYS**
> **TO HEAL IT.** • ROBIN WALL KIMMERER

TAKING CARE OF WHERE WE LIVE

The writer and scientist Robin Wall Kimmerer says that many Indigenous Peoples, like her Potawatomi ancestors, have what is called a culture of gratitude. They are grateful for what the earth provides for them—but they know they are also responsible for contributing to the well-being of the land, sustaining the land that sustains them. The well-being of the land can't be separated from the well-being of both the individual person and the community. This reciprocity is an important part of TEK.

Restoration and rewilding benefit from TEK—from both the knowledge and the reciprocity that it can bring to a project. When scientific knowledge and TEK are used together, both the ecosystem and the culture can be restored, which is good for everyone, human and nonhuman alike! Kimmerer calls restoration that repairs both ecosystems and cultures "reciprocal restoration." It is based on the idea that what's good for the land is good for the people, and what's good for the people is good for the land.

This idea can apply not only to Indigenous Peoples but to settlers as well—the people who settled in the lands of Indigenous Peoples as part of colonization. By learning about TEK, and participating in restoration projects that use TEK, settlers can begin to change their relationship with the land. They can start to understand that *all* people have a responsibility to take care of the places where they live, whether urban or rural, and not just take

CHIIXUU TLL IINASDLL

(NURTURING SEAFOOD TO GROW)

In the 1700s and 1800s, the fur trade wiped out most of the sea-otter population along the entire western coast of North America. (Sea-otter pelts are extremely soft and warm.) Sea otters eat a lot of sea urchins, spiky red shellfish in a food chain that in the Pacific Northwest also included abalone, herring and the sea lions that ate them, salmon and the orcas that ate them—and the people who ate abalone, herring and salmon. When the sea otters were gone, there was nothing to eat the sea urchins, and their population exploded. They ate everything in sight, which eventually destroyed the kelp forests in which they lived.

Kelp forests used to cover a quarter of the world's coastlines, and they are the oceans' most important carbon-capture systems. They provide habitat for thousands of species and capture 20 times more carbon per acre than forests on land. But overfishing (and in the case of the sea otter, overhunting) and warming waters because of climate change are causing the kelp forests to disappear.

Sea otters have been reintroduced in some areas along the coast. But fishermen who rely on sea urchins, abalone and crab don't like the sea otters, and this creates conflict. In Gwaii Haanas National Park Reserve (also a national marine conservation area and Haida heritage site), which is near Xaayda Gwaay (Haida Gwaii), a large group of islands off the north coast of British Columbia, an important restoration project is taking place. It's important not only because it aims to restore a vital ecosystem but also because it is finding a way to do that by combining the traditional knowledge of the Haida First Nation and scientific knowledge—*and* by addressing everyone's needs.

Sea otters haven't been reintroduced in Gwaii Haanas. Instead people are playing the role of sea otters, harvesting and culling the sea urchins themselves, with researchers carefully watching what happens to the rest of the ecosystem. So far what's happening is good—the kelp is growing and other species are returning.

resources from those places. Taking care means respecting the land and water, being grateful for what they provide and actively participating in their well-being.

HEALING ECOSYSTEMS, HEALING OURSELVES

The UN Decade on Ecosystem Restoration may be our best chance to undo some of the harm we've done to the planet, keep climate change manageable and ensure that future generations have a healthy environment to live in. But we have to do it right. If we forget to ask important questions, like who restoration is for and who should do it, we might just make things worse, both for ecosystems and for the people who are part of them. Or, again, to look at the glass half full instead of half empty, we can say that restoration and rewilding that are done well don't just heal ecosystems—they heal us too.

UNITED NATIONS ECOSYSTEM CATEGORY
URBAN AREAS

Urban areas occupy less than 1 percent of the planet's land but are home to more than half of the human population, and that number is expected to continue growing. People who live in towns and cities depend on urban ecosystems—which help clean air and water, reduce temperatures during summer heat and provide places for rest and play, all of which improve urban dwellers' quality of life. Urban ecosystems can also support more biodiversity than you might expect.

Challenges
- Two-thirds of the world's energy consumed and 70 percent of its carbon emissions produced in cities

- Soils paved over or built on, leaving little space for plants and trees
- Air, water and soils polluted by waste and emissions from homes, traffic and industry
- Uncontrolled growth of towns and cities (urban sprawl), destroying plant and animal habitats

Actions We Can Take

- Plant trees and other plants, especially native ones—everywhere!
- Take care of trees and plants by watering during summer heat and drought.
- Restore wetlands and streams, as well as any unused land, such as along roads and railways.
- Ask city planners for more trees and green spaces and more restoration.

RESTORATION SNAPSHOT
CREATING GREEN CORRIDORS IN MEDELLÍN, COLOMBIA

Medellín, the second-largest city in Colombia, has grown rapidly in the last 50 years and is now home to almost four million people. The city was experiencing a severe heat island effect, an increase in temperatures caused by concrete, pavement, buildings and other surfaces absorbing the sun's heat. This extra heat increases energy costs (for air-conditioning) and air pollution, also causing illness and sometimes death.

FIX

The Green Corridors project began in 2016 by training 75 people who were living in poverty to be city gardeners and planting technicians. By 2019 they had planted 80,000 trees and many other plants along 30 corridors—18 roads and 12 waterways—quickly turning them into a network of lush greenery and shade. The city's average temperature had already dropped by 3.6 degrees Fahrenheit (2 degrees Celsius), air pollution was reduced and people's health and well-being improved.

CAN WE REALLY RESTORE URBAN AREAS?

The United Nations includes "urban areas" as one of the eight kinds of ecosystems to be restored during its Decade on Ecosystem Restoration. You might be wondering how a city can be an ecosystem with all that pavement, concrete, steel and glass, and where the most common "organism" is actually a car!

There are lots of ways to restore urban areas. Here are just a few:

It's true that cities and their suburbs might have little or nothing left of the ecosystems in which they were originally built. But most urban areas are built near rivers, lakes or coastal areas, and they may still contain patches of forest or wetland in parks and other public spaces. These remnants can be cleaned up by removing garbage, pollution sources and invasive species, making it possible for native species to return.

Native trees and plants can be planted in public spaces, such as parks and schoolyards, beside roads and railway tracks or under power lines.

Community gardens can be created in empty lots.

On their private property, people can convert lawns to gardens with native trees and plants. Even apartment balconies and rooftops can have plenty of plants and small trees in pots, providing food and habitat for birds and insects.

While some of these efforts might be more like "greening" or "regreening" than actual restoration of the original ecosystems, everything from cleaning up rivers to growing native and other plants in pots can help improve life for humans and other urban inhabitants—providing shade and reducing temperatures, and cleaning air and water.

NOT JUST A WALK IN THE PARK

Urban restoration does face challenges, though, and not just ecological ones. The biggest challenges for restoring urban ecosystems can involve people. As we've seen, good restoration always begins with consulting everyone who might be affected. In the case of a public urban area, like a park, this will include a *lot* of people, and they will have a lot of different ideas about what should happen there, which can create conflict.

Another social challenge for urban restoration is making sure that it happens in all kinds of neighborhoods, not just the wealthier ones. That has been a problem in the past, and it's another form of environmental racism. All communities should have the opportunity to be involved in and benefit from restoration.

Restoration is for everyone!

CONFLICT? WHAT CONFLICT?

If you live in a town or city, you can probably think of a nearby park, maybe with a bit of grass and some trees. It's nice, right? Nice—until this happens: The people with dogs want to let their dogs be unleashed. People with children and no dogs don't want dogs unleashed, and neither do people who want native plants, which can't be trampled, in the park. Lots of people, with or without children or dogs, will want grass that is regularly watered and mowed, but people who want native plants will want to get rid of at least some of the grass. Some people will want trees for shade, and sunbathers will want no shade. People who use the park at night might not want trees for safety reasons. And...you get the idea!

CHAPTER FIVE
ACTING

It's time to act.

In order to slow climate change and avoid losing much of the planet's biodiversity, ecosystems covering a large area of the earth need to be protected and restored. We all need to do what we can. But it sure can feel overwhelming: What to do? How? Where? When?

Here are some ideas to help get you started.

> ❝ **HOPE DOESN'T COME FROM WORDS.** ❞
> **HOPE ONLY COMES FROM ACTIONS.**
> • GRETA THUNBERG

Buying food from local farmers markets is a better way to consume—not only by reducing emissions that contribute to climate change but also by supporting the local economy.

RAWPIXELIMAGES/DREAMSTIME.COM

FIND WAYS TO CONSUME LESS AND CONSUME BETTER

We need to start taking less from the earth. Everything we buy starts from the earth in one way or another—and returns to the earth. Here are two examples that might surprise you.

WILD IDEA

As much as 30 percent of all the food produced around the world is wasted. When food rots in landfills, it releases greenhouse gases like methane into the atmosphere. Scientists estimate that food waste accounts for as much as 10 percent of human-caused greenhouse gas emissions.

WHERE YOUR FOOD COMES FROM— AND WHERE IT GOES

The way we eat can have a big impact not just on our own health but on the planet's. The beef patty in your burger or the meat you buy at the grocery store might be coming from land that has been cleared in the Amazon rainforest or elsewhere, contributing to biodiversity loss and the release of carbon into the atmosphere. Eating a more plant-based diet, and eating foods that are produced locally and seasonally, can reduce our impact on the planet in several different ways, from reducing emissions that contribute to climate change to using less water.

Reducing the amount of food we waste can also have a positive impact, for at least two reasons. If we waste less, we don't have to produce as much. We can stop converting forests and grasslands to agricultural land and stop overharvesting in oceans and freshwaters. And less waste in landfills means fewer emissions of greenhouse gases (chemicals in the atmosphere that contribute to climate change).

WHERE YOUR JEANS COME FROM— AND WHERE THEY END UP

You probably have at least one pair of blue jeans, right? Consider this:

- The cotton they're made of needs huge amounts of water and chemicals to grow.

- They were likely made in a sweatshop that pays people, and sometimes children, low wages for long hours of work in poor conditions.

- The blue dye and other toxic chemicals used in the dyeing process are often dumped in rivers.

- It takes about 1,000 gallons (3,785 liters) of water to make one pair of jeans. (Denim with that cool "distressed" look uses even more chemicals—and more water.)

- Each time you wash your jeans, tiny fibers from the fabric (called microfibers) get flushed out and are too small to be filtered by wastewater treatment plants, so they end up in rivers, lakes and oceans. Scientists have even found them in the Arctic, thousands of miles from any human activity.

- And, of course, when our jeans are no longer wearable, they end up in the landfill, which is another problem.

DO I REALLY NEED THIS?

We can use the same questions about buying jeans for everything we buy, from clothing to electronic devices to vehicles. Do I really need this? Can I keep using my old one or borrow one from someone? If not, is there a version that uses fewer resources, produces less waste and treats people better? You might need to do some research first, but you'll always learn something interesting when you do!

Water filled with toxic chemicals used in nearby jeans factories is used by local farmers growing corn in Tehuacán, Mexico.
ERIC DEMERS

You're probably not going to live your life without another pair of blue jeans. But the next time you go to buy a new pair, pause for a moment. Could you alter or mend the ones you have to make them last longer? Could you buy a secondhand pair or pay a bit more for a brand with a smaller environmental and social impact? Could you give your old ones to someone else rather than throwing them away?

FIND WAYS TO BE MORE BIOCENTRIC

Even if you live in the middle of a large city, you can start being more biocentric—thinking of yourself and your community as part of a local ecosystem, and a global ecosystem, in which everything you do affects everything else, both in the

moment and in the future. Wherever you are, you can start by noticing the other living things around you—even the weeds poking through a broken sidewalk or the pigeons perching on a telephone wire are alive, have value and are interesting. Be curious. Take time just to look and listen. What is that squirrel up to? What kind of tree is that? Where is that bee going? Which bird is that singing?

Another important thing you can do is find out about the ground under your feet. There's a good chance that the land on which your home is built was stolen from Indigenous people. Do you know who those people are and where they live today? If not, try to learn more about them. Noticing and learning about the natural world in which you live, and acknowledging the people on whose land you stand, can be the first steps toward truly belonging in a place. Belonging means both giving and receiving—not just taking—and recognizing that we have responsibilities for the well-being of that place.

Know the history of the place where you live. How can you contribute to the well-being of that place?
RENA SCHILD/SHUTTERSTOCK.COM

UNITED NATIONS ECOSYSTEM CATEGORY
MOUNTAINS

Mountains are found on every continent and take up about a quarter of the planet's land. They aren't a single ecosystem but many different ones, which hold not only a great deal of biodiversity (about half of the world's biodiversity hotspots) but also a lot of cultural diversity—cultures that have found different ways to survive in often difficult conditions. Mountains are also known as the "water towers of the world," supplying fresh water for about half of the world's human population.

Challenges

- Easily damaged by human activities and climate change
- Serious erosion caused by clearing forests on steep mountain slopes, in turn affecting water that people depend on farther down the slopes
- Amounts of water flowing down the slopes affected by climate change, sometimes causing flooding below
- Delicate ecosystems in already harsh mountain conditions severely affected by rising temperatures

Actions We Can Take

- Restore forests on mountain slopes to reduce erosion and help prevent landslides, avalanches and floods.
- Use resources wisely, and use sustainable practices like agroforestry to help ecosystems and people adjust to the changing climate.

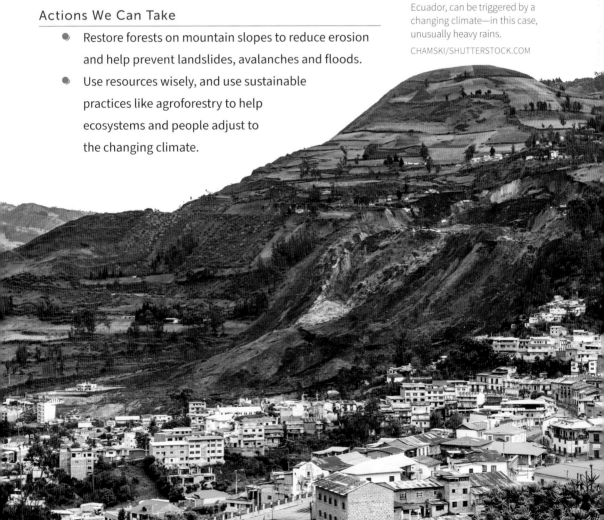

Landslides, like this one in Alausi, Ecuador, can be triggered by a changing climate—in this case, unusually heavy rains.
CHAMSKI/SHUTTERSTOCK.COM

RESTORATION SNAPSHOT
THREE CONTINENTS, FOUR COUNTRIES, MANY MOUNTAINS

Mountain ecosystems are often fragile, and climate change is making the conditions in which they have evolved even harsher. Around the world, glaciers on mountaintops are melting. The water running off the mountains is eroding mountainsides already weakened by over-grazing. And the water supply that cities and farms on the plains below rely on is becoming too much or too little.

FIX

The Multi-Country Mountain Initiative is one of the United Nations' World Restoration Flagships, which are considered the best examples of restoration affecting large areas long into the future. By teaming up and sharing what they've learned, Kyrgyzstan (Asia), Serbia (Eastern Europe) and Uganda and Rwanda (Africa) are reviving their mountain ecosystems, making them more resilient so the can continue to deliver their benefits to people—and support their unique wildlife.

In Kyrgyzstan, grasslands are being managed to provide better food for live-stock and Asiatic ibex. With the return of the ibex, their predator, the snow leopard, is slowly returning. In Serbia, two nature parks preserve valuable pastures and restored and expanded forests. And in Uganda and Rwanda, which share one of only two remaining populations of the endangered mountain gorilla protection of the gorillas' habitat with the help of local communities has helped double the gorilla population in the last 30 years. It has also supported a new tourism industry, which created jobs and other economic opportunities.

RESTORE AND REWILD

Of course, this book couldn't end without urging you to get involved—in whatever ways you can—in healing the ecosystems that you live within or near. Be part of Generation Restoration!

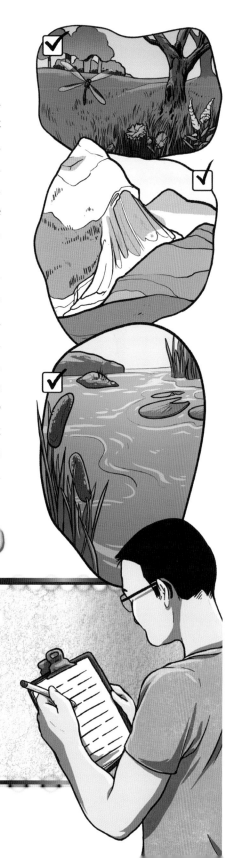

If you are lucky enough to live in a home with a yard, ask your parents or guardian if you can plant some native plants and trees. You should be able to find out online what the native plants in your region are, and which ones will best suit the conditions of your yard. Or talk to your teacher about starting a patch of native plants at school. Be sure to take care of what you plant, or what has been planted before.

Searching online for restoration or rewilding projects in your area should lead you to at least one organization that is restoring a nearby wetland or park, beach or river, grassland or forest. Projects like these often rely on volunteers for removing invasive plant species, planting native ones and other important tasks. Some groups meet regularly, so you can get to know other people with interests like yours. You'll also learn about plants and animals in your area, and, if Indigenous people are involved, you might have the chance to learn from them.

NAME THOSE ECOSYSTEMS!

If you live in a rural area, you might be lucky enough to have several ecosystems right outside your door. Even if you live in a big city, you might be surprised by how many there are nearby. Is there a river or a lake in your city, or is it on the shore of an ocean? Is there a forest nearby or even just a patch of forest? Can you see mountains from where you are? Is there farmland outside the town or city limits? Once you've identified them, you can start to find out more about them.

Take time to look. What's growing around you?
ANNA LIGHT/SHUTTERSTOCK.COM

By participating in well-planned restoration projects, you will be helping repair the planet. But you'll also be changing your own relationship with nature, by learning, caring and giving back. Healing the earth, we heal ourselves.

WILD IDEA

Are you on social media? Tag your posts about restoration and rewilding activities with #GenerationRestoration so others in the movement can find you.

#Generation Restoration

GLOSSARY

agroforestry—a type of farming in which trees are grown together with crops and livestock

biocentric—seeing humans as just one species among many in an ecosystem, and nonhuman things as valuable in and of themselves, not just as resources for humans to exploit

biodiversity—the variety and variability of living things in an ecosystem

biodiversity hotspots—regions with a large number of plant species that grow nowhere else in the world and that are under threat from things like development, pollution and disease

book of Genesis—part of both the Tanakh (Hebrew Bible) and the Christian Bible

climate change—changes in weather patterns, caused by human activity

conservation—the science and practice of protecting and preserving ecosystems and biodiversity

cultural keystone species—a plant or animal that plays an essential part in the life and culture of a community

degradation—damage through misuse or overuse by humans

disturbance—a natural event or human activity that benefits or harms an ecosystem

ecological restoration—the science and practice of assisting in the recovery of ecosystems that have been degraded, damaged or destroyed

ecologist—a scientist who studies ecology, or the relationships between organisms and their environment

economy—the system through which we produce, buy and sell goods and services

ecosystem—a community of living and nonliving things that share the same habitat and are connected in many ways

ecosystem restoration—see *ecological restoration*

ecosystem services—the many benefits that humans receive from healthy ecosystems

Enlightenment—the so-called age of reason, a period of intense scientific, political and philosophical dialogue in 18th-century Europe

environmental justice—the fair treatment and inclusion of all people, with respect to developing and enforcing environmental laws and policies, to ensure that everyone can live, work, play and learn in a healthy environment

environmental racism—decisions and practices of governments and corporations that target racialized and marginalized communities for polluting industries and toxic waste

erosion—the wearing away of soil and other materials by water, wind and the impacts of forest clearing and poor agricultural practices

estuaries—places where freshwater rivers meet the salty tidal water of oceans

exotic species—plants or animals that are introduced into areas where they don't occur naturally

food chain—the sequence of who eats whom in an ecosystem; all the food chains in an ecosystem form a **food web**

food security—when all people have access to food that meets all their needs; **food insecurity** is the opposite

grasslands—large areas dominated by grasses

habitat—the place where a plant or animal normally lives

Industrial Revolution—a period of economic and social change that began in England in 1760 with the shift to machine-made items and large factories

invasive species—a plant or animal species (usually exotic) that spreads and causes problems when it is moved (usually by humans) to a new place

keystone species—a plant or animal that has a much larger effect on an ecosystem than all the others in it

mangroves—trees and shrubs that grow in salt water on the coasts of tropical and subtropical regions

mass extinction—an event in which a large proportion of Earth's species die out in a relatively short time

monocultures—single crops grown over large areas and for a long time

native species—plants or animals that have evolved in a place without help from humans

organism—a living thing, such as a plant, animal, insect, fish, fungus, virus or bacterium

Pleistocene rewilding—reintroducing large animals similar to those that went extinct during the Ice Age, to solve ecological problems

settlers—people who move to a new place as part of colonial policy to take control of that place and its people in order to exploit its resources

wetlands—areas of land where the soil is either covered with water or saturated with water for all or part of the year

RESOURCES

BOOKS

Briggs Martin, Jacqueline. *Creekfinding: A True Story*. University of Minnesota Press, 2017.

Drake, Jane, and Ann Love. *Rewilding: Giving Nature a Second Chance*. Annick Press, 2017.

Gornish, Elise. *A Kids Guide to Ecological Restoration*. Author, 2022.

Ignotofsky, Rachel. *The Wondrous Workings of Planet Earth: Understanding Our World and Its Ecosystems*. Ten Speed Press, 2018.

Klein, Naomi, with Rebecca Stefoff. *How to Change Everything: The Young Human's Guide to Protecting the Planet and Each Other*. Atheneum Books for Young Readers, 2021.

Leopold, Aldo. *A Sand County Almanac: And Sketches Here and There*. Oxford University Press, 1949, 2020.

Lerwill, Ben. *Climate Rebels*. Puffin, 2021.

Steen, David A., and Chiara Fedele. *Rewilding: Bringing Wildlife Back Where It Belongs*. St. Martin's Press, 2022.

VIDEOS

Ecology Transforms Youth: youthecology.ca

Restore: Films from the Frontiers of Hope: decadeonrestoration.org/restore-films-frontiers-hope

WEBSITES

Jane Goodall Institute: janegoodall.org

Jane Goodall Institute of Canada: janegoodall.ca

Knepp: knepp.co.uk

Make a Difference Week: makeadifferenceweek.org

Panthera: panthera.org

Planet-Based Diets: planetbaseddiets.panda.org

Regreening Africa: regreeningafrica.org

Re:wild: rewild.org

Roots and Shoots: rootsandshoots.org

The World Counts: theworldcounts.com

United Nations Decade on Ecosystem Restoration: decadeonrestoration.org

Wild Foundation: wild.org

World Wildlife Fund: worldwildlife.org

Youth and Ecological Restoration: youthecology.ca

Links to external resources are for personal and/or educational use only and are provided in good faith without any express or implied warranty. There is no guarantee given as to the accuracy or currency of any individual item. The author and publisher provide links as a service to readers. This does not imply any endorsement by the author or publisher of any of the content accessed through these links.

ACKNOWLEDGMENTS

First, to the Lekwungen Peoples, whose Traditional Territory is the beautiful southern tip of Vancouver Island, where I am lucky enough to live, háy'sxʷ q̓ə!

As always, my thanks to Orca for continuing to make books on challenging topics. And to my editor, Kirstie Hudson, for your enthusiasm (always) and for your patience and support (this time especially); to designer Troy Cunningham and illustrator Amanda Key for bringing this book to life.

Special thanks to Kristen Miskelly, biologist and ecological restorationist extraordinaire, for her excellent suggestions and her meadow-making guidance generally. Thanks also to Suzanne Methot for her sensitive reading and illuminating suggestions.

I am grateful to those who have been my teachers in ecological restoration, whether directly or indirectly, including Eric Higgs at the University of Victoria and Robin Wall Kimmerer. Thank you for leading the way.

And finally, to my family, thank you for supporting my serial obsessions, and especially to Christopher, for the budding, buzzing, messy restoration project that is our garden.

INDEX

PAGE NUMBERS IN **BOLD** INDICATE AN IMAGE CAPTION.

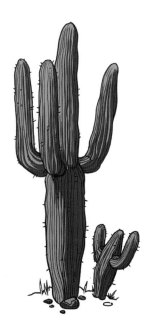

ORCA Think

THE MORE YOU KNOW...

ALL CONSUMING
SHOP SMARTER FOR THE PLANET

LET'S GET CREATIVE
ART FOR A HEALTHY PLANET

JESSICA ROSE   ILLUSTRATED BY JARETT SITTER

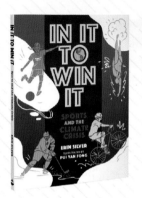

IN IT TO WIN IT
SPORTS AND THE CLIMATE CRISIS

ERIN SILVER
ILLUSTRATED BY PUI YAN FONG

ALONE TOGETHER
A CURIOUS EXPLORATION OF LONELINESS

BETTI FONG
ILLUSTRATED BY JONATHAN DYCK

REMEMBER THIS
The Fascinating World of Memory

Monique Polak   Illustrated by Valéry Goulet

OPEN SCIENCE
KNOWLEDGE FOR EVERYONE

MONIQUE POLAK
ILLUSTRATED BY CATHERINE CHAN

GOOD FOOD, BAD WASTE
Let's Eat for the Planet

Erin Silver   Illustrated by Suharu Ogawa

BREAKING NEWS
WHY MEDIA MATTERS

RAINA DELISLE
Illustrated by Julie McLaughlin

SAVE NATURAL HABITATS!!

EQUALITY = FOR = ALL

Right to Live Free of Discrimination

RIGHT to SPeAK UP!

RIGHT TO LIVE

RIGHT TO LEARN

THE MORE YOU GROW

Tanya Lloyd Kyi / Julia Kyi
BETTER CONNECTED
How Girls Are Using Social Media for Good

Jen Sookfong Lee
FINDING HOME
The Journey of Immigrants and Refugees
ILLUSTRATED BY Drew Shannon

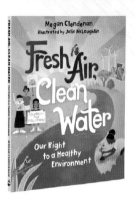

Megan Clendenan / illustrated by Julie McLaughlin
Fresh Air, Clean Water
Our Right to a Healthy Environment

GET OUT AND VOTE!
How You Can Shape the Future
Elizabeth MacLeod / Illustrated by Emily Chu

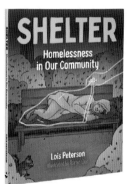

SHELTER
Homelessness in Our Community
Lois Peterson

SUPERPOWER?
The Wearable-Tech Revolution
ELAINE KACHALA / Illustrated by BELLE WUTHRICH

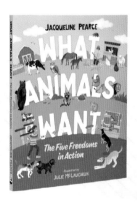

JACQUELINE PEARCE
WHAT ANIMALS WANT
The Five Freedoms in Action
Illustrated by JULIE McLAUGHLIN

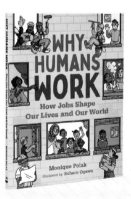

WHY HUMANS WORK
How Jobs Shape Our Lives and Our World
Monique Polak / illustrated by Suharu Ogawa

WHAT'S THE BIG IDEA? The **Orca Think** series introduces us to the issues making headlines in the world today. It encourages us to question, connect and take action for a better future. With those tools we can all become better citizens. Now that's smart thinking!

PHOTO CREDIT: MARYAM MORRISON

MERRIE-ELLEN WILCOX is a writer and editor in Victoria, British Columbia. She is the author of *What's the Buzz?* and *Nature Out of Balance* in the Orca Footprints series. When she's not at her desk or reading books, she's usually working in her garden, watching bees and birds, and planting even more native plants. She studied ecological restoration at the University of Victoria.

PHOTO CREDIT: JOHN GARDINER

AMANDA KEY is is an illustrator and graphic designer from Nanaimo, British Columbia. Her art centers around the natural landscape of Vancouver Island and draws from her childhood spent finding flowers, hiking trails and spotting animals. With a strong focus on observation and natural science, each design piece offers a chance to learn a bit more about her surroundings.